S HERETICUS ORDONI MAGI ALCAZAN OCCULTIST
NCT WARRANT MILITANTE TECHNOGRAP
ROTELEPATH PREFECTI METATRON MUNI
ER PROCLAMATOR FAMULOUS DIALOGOUS ENFORCER
NIST MATERIUM ASPIRANT REDEMTIONIST REDEMPTORII
YBERSEER BONESEER MUTANI DEATHE MASKA PSYKER
TUS TECHNOMAT TAROTSCRIOR DARK SCION MYSTIC
ALPHAS ENSLAYER SCAVENGER COMMISSAR SCHOLE
EDICANTUS MENDICANTE REVISIONIST WATCHMAN
GALLOWGLASS FAUVILLE EXCRUCIATOR GOVENOR
OMANCER STIRLITE HYPAPYSTON HAGG BOT NANOPHYLII
OR SERVENTO LOGI VIGILODE IMPERORITE INQUISITOR
ATHCORE LEVINE CORTTEWAYNE ALCHEMIST STARKKYND
OT ACCOLYTUS CUSTODIAN BLACK GUARD OVERLORD
NGMAN CUTSTOVE HEADSMAN ADAPTII HENCHMAN
CHRONO GLADIATOR PROPHECT SEER SAGE STEERSMAN
STRYKE CUTTAR PATHFINDER WAYSMITH JURYCANT LOCK
UE TRADER DEATH CULTIST SUN SLINGER MULTICHMIST
EKER NAVIGATOR MECHANIK RENEGADE TECHPRIEST
MAGES CARYATID TALLYMAN DESPERADO CONFESSOR
MASTER LEXOGRAPHER LOGISTER WARP STEALER INDITT
EST SOLAR PRIEST VYPERION CULT MECHAN TECH ADEPT
RMITE CHAPLAIN DIOCESAN PRELATE PULPITEER SEXTANT
GUNNE MERCANTILIST JOURNEY MAN SARGEANT AT ARMS
SISTER DICISPLINATOR APOSTATE NOMAD HIVER SHADOW

OMNISSIAH MAGOS BLESSED ALCHEMY ORDINA
THAUMATURGE WARLOCK JUSTICAR OBSCURINE AD
PRIEST MECH DEACON POTENTIATE CONFEDERATE
PHYSISCIA INTERROGATER PUPPETEER DRONE TARGE
REGULATOR PROCTOR MARSHALL LORD HIGH LORD AI
NEONATE SANCTIONITE MECHWRIGHT ENGINSEER
SCOURGE KYNG DESPERADO THRONE AGENT PREF
WARRIOR FAMILIAR SAVANT WARPSEER EXPLICATO
PROGENUMATE CREEDYTE ORATOR SUPPLICANTER
GARROWGATOR HARROWHOUND CATAPHRACT
XENOSTERENNE NEUROMAUNCHER DIGI MAUNCER XE
STROOGEMENNE BRETHRENDAE ANCHORITE ADORA
PURITAN ACOLYTE RADICAL ASSASSIN JUDGE ARBITES
GUNNJAK HOBBLON PYCKESPUR SLAYER SHACKLEM
CHIROGEONNE GREY GUARDIAN EXECUTIONER F
HIEROPHANT ARGOFLAGGELLANT STAGTOSSI CRUCIBLA
AELMJAK BOG FERREL NIGHT CUR WEAPONSMITH SUN
STAUNCH CRUSADER ZEALOT KEY KEEPER MALLEON R
BOUNTY HUNTER HYRDMANNE ASTROPATH ASTO
MECHONPERITTE REPENTIANS BURNING MARTYR AR
SEVITOR SERVADON DUELIST CLERIC ARBITRATOR LOI
CHIRUGEON SCRIBE SCRIVONOR MISSIONARY HELIO
CABALYTE ADJUNDANT ANNIHALATOR ILLUMINATOR F
SKINNER XENOGRAPHER BATTLE BISHOP GUILDER FRE
THYBILANT PILGRIM HADIANT APOSTICATOR SORORITA

THE EMPEROR'S WILL

COMPILED BY JOHN BLANCHE

For ten thousand years the Emperor of Mankind has sat immobile upon his Golden Throne. Through all that century of centuries he has uttered not a single word nor made any gesture of command. His desiccated corpse-like figure shows no sign of life as it is normally understood. The faint pulsing of preservative ichor being pumped through his shrivelled veins is the only movement a studious observer could discern. In like manner, the Emperor's thoughts remain unknown and unknowable, his mind is ever silent and closed to telepathic enquiry. The cryptic predictions gleaned from the Emperor's Tarot and the Astronomican continuing to broadcast its unwavering signal are taken as proof enough that the Emperor prevails and that he has not yet surrendered to his seeming fate and abandoned humanity altogether.

How then is the Imperium of Mankind guided through the grim darkness of the 41st Millennium? If not at the literal command of the Emperor, then how is humanity able to face the perils that encircle it and gnaw at it from within? What power exists in the universe that can wield the Emperor's might and do his bidding? The myriad agents and officers of the Imperium's great institutions are that very power. From highborn noble Lord of the Inquisition to deadly assassin snatched from some hive world gutter, men and women of savage faith, warriors, priests, judges, jurists and executioners: each and every one of them wields a tiny, but nevertheless potent, fraction of the Emperor's authority. To them is given the gravest responsibility: to enact the Emperor's Will.

omnissiah magos blessed alchemy ordinatus
hereticus ordoni magi alcazan occultist thaumaturge
warlock justicar obscurine warrant-militantte
technographer electro-priest mech deacon
potentiate confederate astrotelepath prefecti
metatron munitori healer physiscia interrogator
puppeteer drone targeteer proclamator famulous
dialogous enforcer regulator proctor marshall lord
high lord arcanist materium aspirant redemptionist
redemptorii neonate sanctionite mechwright
enginseer cyberseer boneseer mutanti
deathe-maska psyker scourge-kyng desperado
throne agent prefectus technomat tarotscrior

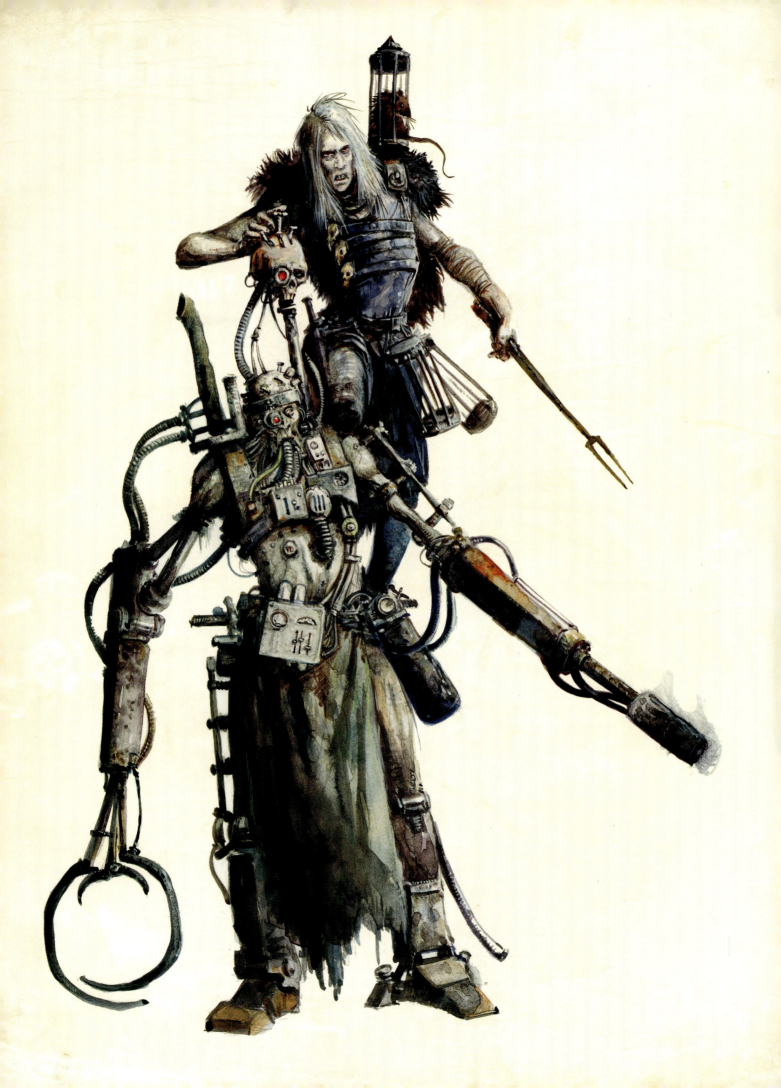

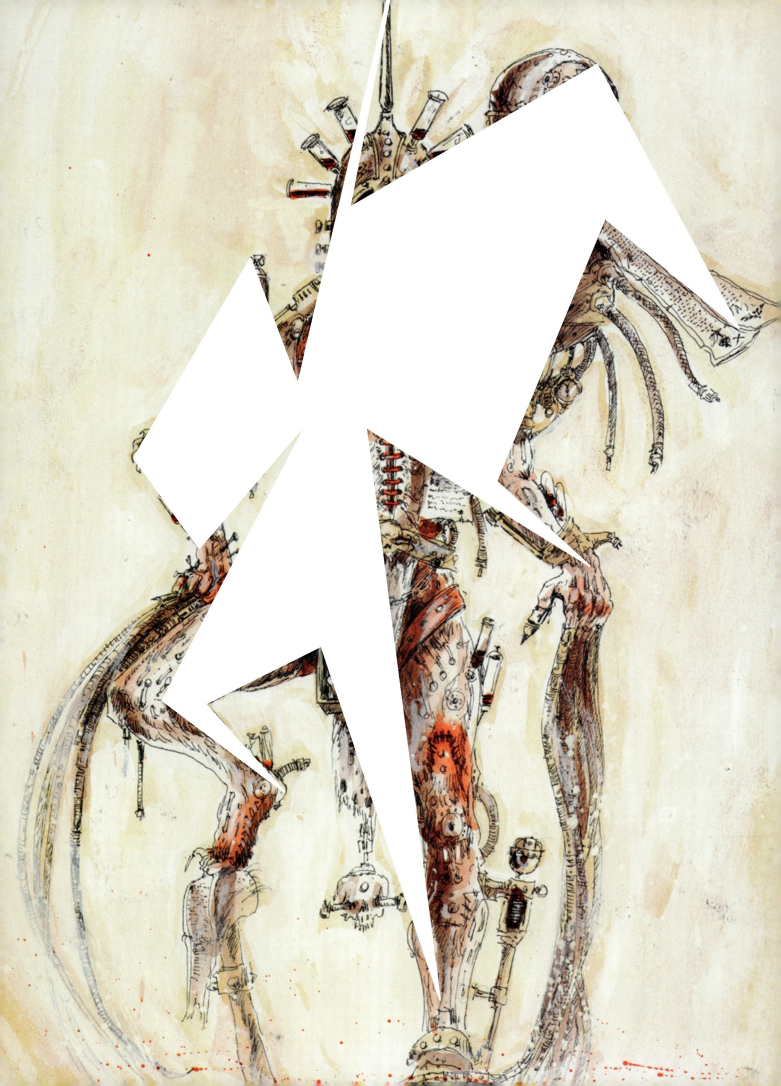

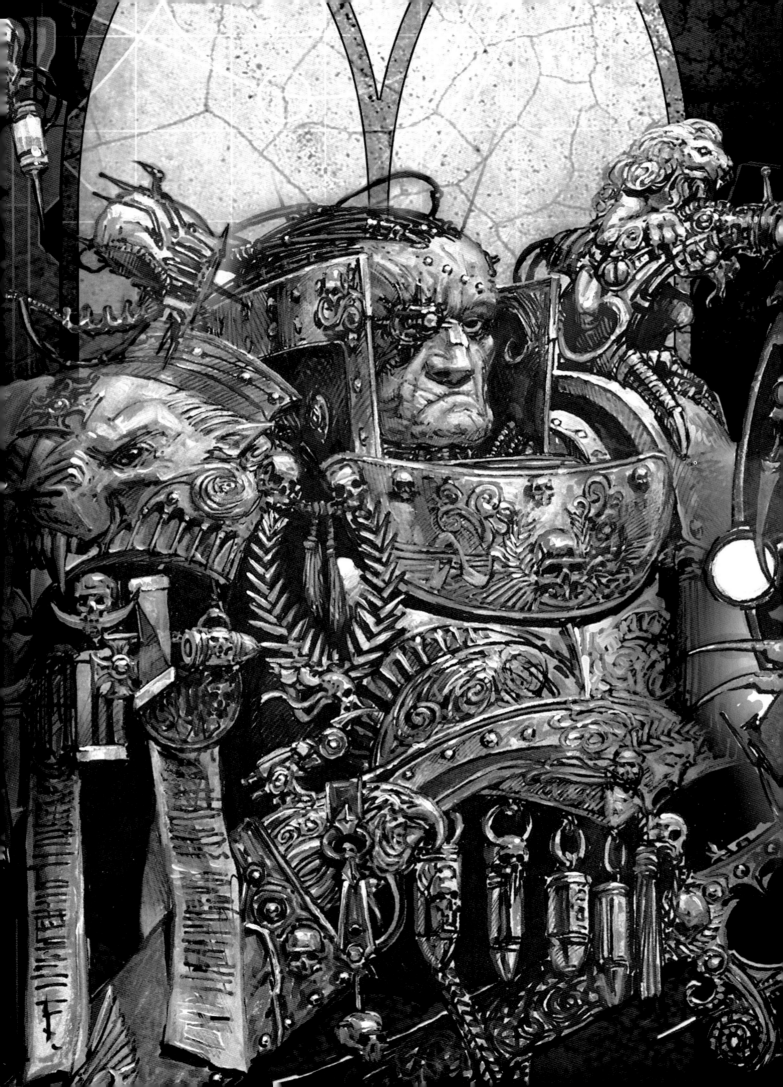

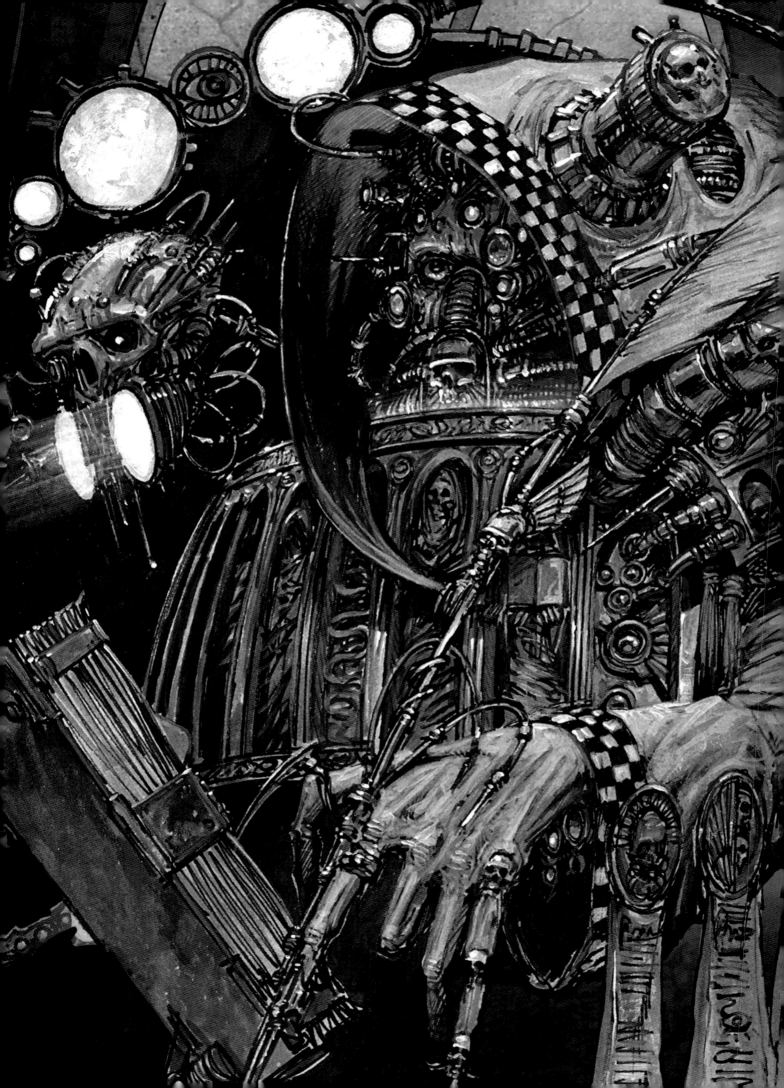

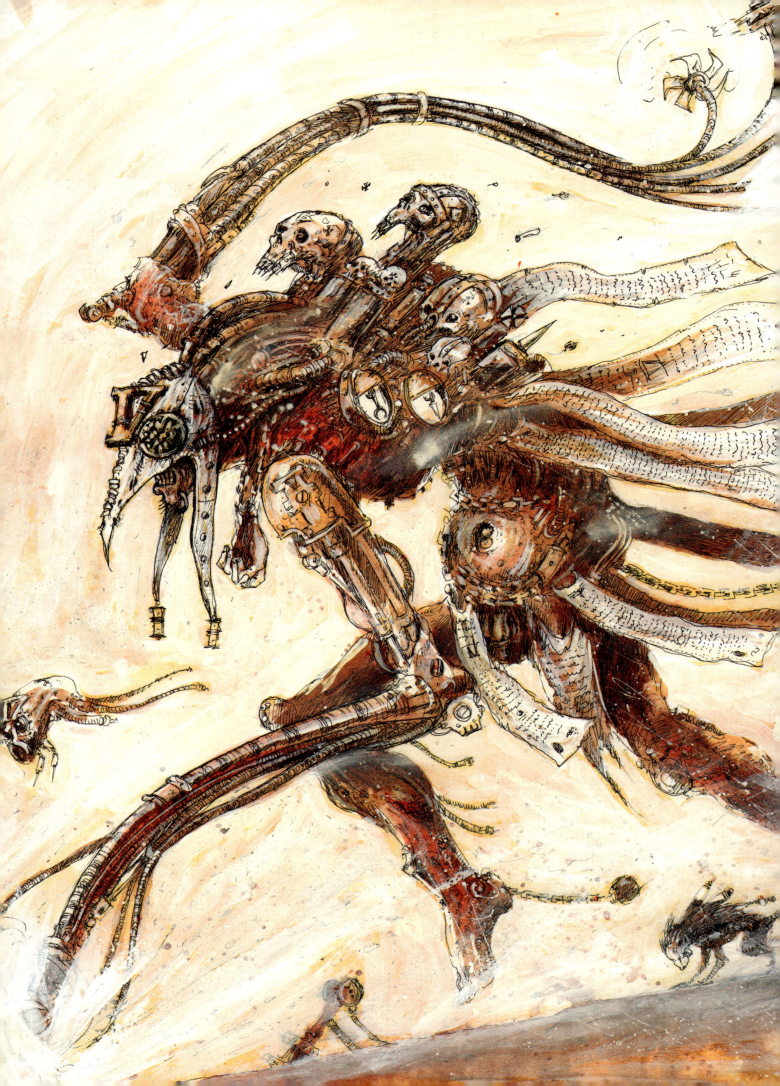

shacklemoot accolytus custodian black guard overlord chirogeonne grey guardian executioner hangman cutstove headsman adaptii henchman hierophant arco-flagellant stagiossi cruciblast chrono-gladiator prophect seer sage steersman aelmjak bog-ferrel night-cur weaponsmith sunn-stryke cuttar pathfinder waysmith jurycant lock-staunch crusader zealot key-keeper malleon rogue trader death cultist gun-slinger multichemist bounty hunter hyrdmanne astropath astoseeker navigator mechanik renegade techpriest mechonperitte repentians burning martyr arch-mages caryatid tallyman desperado confessor

dark scion mystic warrior familiar savant warpseer explicator alphas enslaver scavenger commissar schole progeiumate creedyte orator supplicanter medicantus mendicante revisionist watchman garrowgator harrowhound cataphractus gallowglass fauville excruciator governor xenosterenne neuromauncer digimauncer xenomauncer stirlite hypapyston haggbot nanophylii stroogemenne brethrendae anchorite adorator servento logi vigilode imperorite inquisitor puritan acolyte radical assassin judge arbites deathcore levine corttewayne alchemist starkkynd gunnjak hobblon pyckespur slayer shacklemoot accolytus

dark scion mystic
warrior familiar
savant warpseer
explicator alphas
enslaver scavenger
commissar schole
progeiumate creedyte
orator supplicanter
medicantus mendicante
revisionist watchman
garrowgator
harrowhound
cataphractus
gallowglass fauville
excruciator governor
xenosterenne
neuromauncer
digimauncer
xenomancer stirlite
hypapyston
haggbot nanophylii
stroogemenne
brethrendae anchorite
adorator servento-logi
vigilode imperorite
inquisitor puritan
acolyte radical assassin
judge arbites deathcore
Levine corttewayne
alchemist starkkynd
gunnjak hobblon
pyckespur slayer
shacklemoot accolytus
custodian black guard
overlord chirogeonne
grey guardian
executioner hangman
cutstove headsman
adaptii henchman
hierophant
arco-flagellant stagiossi
cruciblast
chrono-gladiator
prophect seer sage
steersman aelmjak

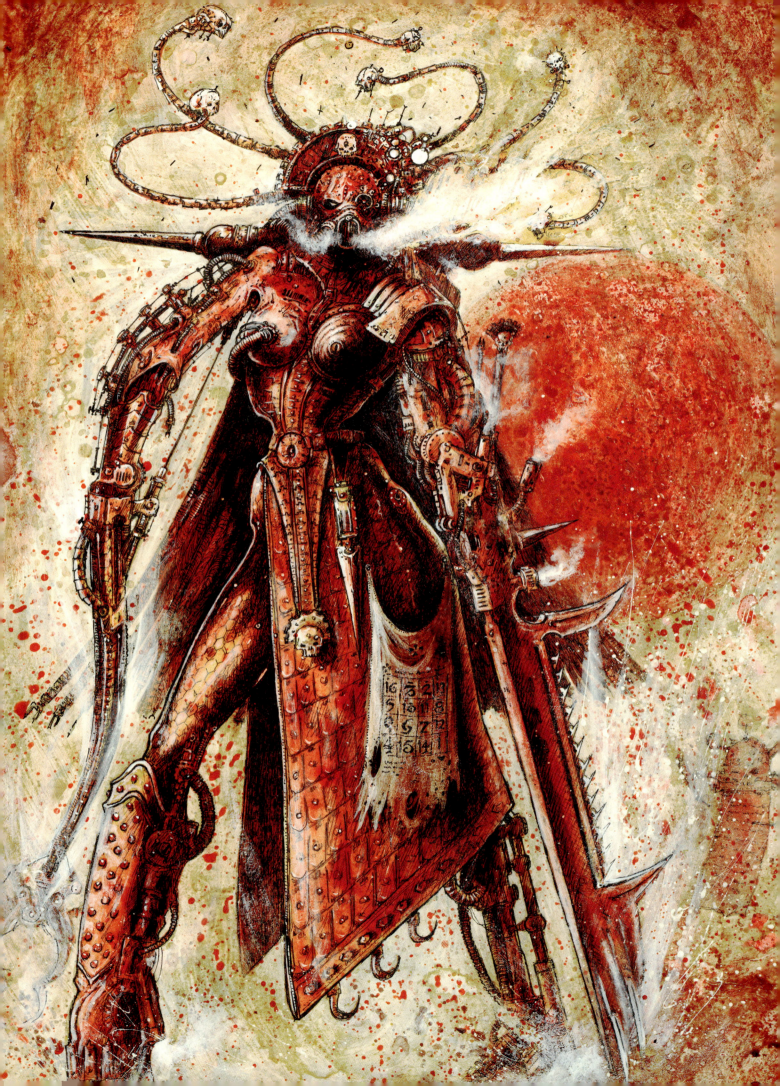

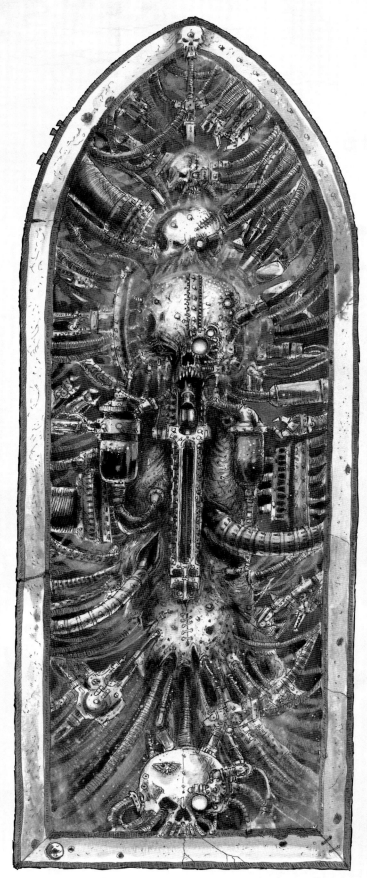

sage steersman aelmjak bog-ferrel night-cur weaponsmith sunn-stryke cuttar pathfinder waysmith jurycant lock-staunch crusader zealot key-keeper malleon rogue trader death cultist gun-slinger multichemist bounty hunter hyrdmanne astropath astoseeker navigator mechanik renegade techpriest mechonperitte repentians burning martyr arch-mages caryatid tallyman desperado confessor servitor servadon duelist cleric arbitrator lore-master lexographer logister warp-stealer inditt chirugeon scribe scrivener annihilator

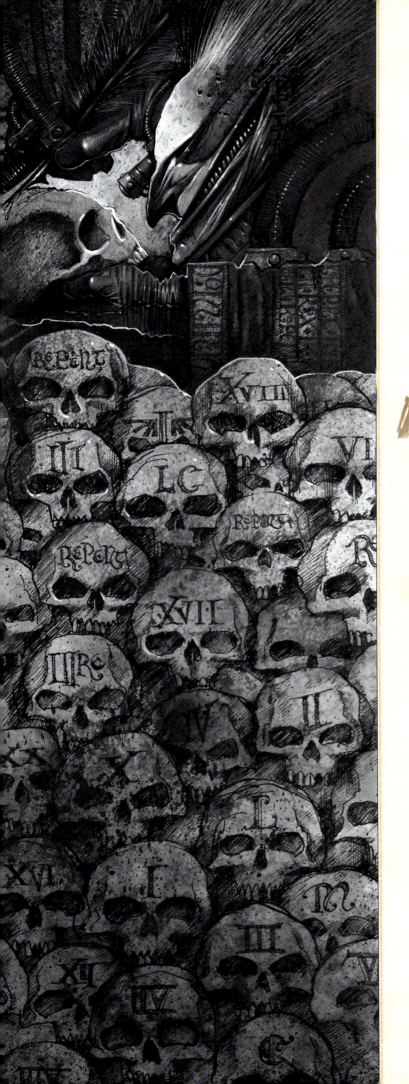

helio-priest solar-priest
vyperion cult-mechan
tech-adept cabalyte
adjundant annihilator
illuminator hermite
chaplain diocesan prelate
pulpiteer sextant skinner
xenographer
battle-bishop guilder
free gunne mercantilist
journey-man
sergeant-at-arms
thybilant pilgrim hadiant
aposticator sororitan
sister dicisplinator
apostate nomad hiver
shadow nobli stygiast
wayfarer settler diviner
elder friar holyman
anchorite cenobite
champion omnissiah
magos blessed alchemyst
ordinatus hereticus
ordoni magii alcazan
occultist thaumaturge

prefecti metatron
munitori healer
physiscia interrogator
puppeteer drone targeteer
proclamator famulous
dialogous enforcer
regulator proctor
marshall lord
high lord arcanist
materium aspirant
redemptionist
redemptorii neonate
sanctionite mechwright
enginseer cyberseer
boneseer mutanti
deathe-maska psyker
scourge-kyng desperado
throne agent prefectus
technomat tarotscrior
dark scion mystic warrior
familiar savant warpseer
explicator alphas enslaver
scavenger commissar
schole progeiumate
creedyte orator
supplicanter medicantus

 A Black Library Production

CREDITS

Art compiled and designed by John Blanche
Graphics and layout by Adrian Wood
Introduction by Alan Merrett

ILLUSTRATIONS

John Blanche, Alex Boyd, Matt Bradbury, Kevin Chin, Paul Dainton, Wayne England, David Gallagher, Jes Goodwin, Igor Kieryluk, Clint Langley, Will Rees, Adrian Smith and Andrea Uderzo

ADDITIONAL GRAPHICS
Marcus Trenkner

Special thanks to Fantasy Flight Games

Thanks to Zaff Haydn-Davies

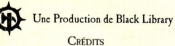 Une Production de Black Library

CRÉDITS

Sélection et design par John Blanche
Graphisme et mise en page par Adrian Wood
Introduction par Alan Merrett

ILLUSTRATIONS

John Blanche, Alex Boyd, Matt Bradbury, Kevin Chin, Paul Dainton, Wayne England, David Gallagher, Jes Goodwin, Igor Kieryluk, Clint Langley, Will Rees, Adrian Smith et Andrea Uderzo

GRAPHISMES ADDITIONNELS
Marcus Trenkner

Remerciements spéciaux Fantasy Flight Games

Remerciements Zaff Haydn-Davies

UK ISBN 13: 978-1-84970-113-6   US ISBN 13: 978-1-84970-114-3
GW UK Product code: 60100181182 US Product code: 70100181182
A Black Library publication. This book published by the Black Library, Games Workshop Ltd, Willow Road, Lenton, Nottingham NG7 2WS, UK.
© Games Workshop Limited 2011. All rights reserved.

Find out more about the Black Library at: www.blacklibrary.com.
Find out more about Games Workshop and the worlds of Warhammer 40,000 at: www.games-workshop.com.
Alternatively, call our mail order hotlines on 0115 - 91 40 000 (UK) or 1-800-394-GAME (US).
Printed in China.

ISBN Francais: 978-1-78030-031-3
GW France Product code : 01100181015
Une publication Black Library. Ce livre est publié par Black Library, Games Workshop Ltd, Willow Road, Lenton, Nottingham NG7 2WS, UK.
© Games Workshop Limited 2011. Tous Droits réservés.

Plus d'informations sur Black Library en Français sur www.blacklibrary.com/france
Plus d'informations sur Games Workshop et Warhammer 40,000 sur www.games-workshop.com.
Vous pouvez aussi nous contacter au 0 442 903 838.
Imprimé en Chine.

S HERETICUS ORDONI MAGI ALCAZAN OCCULTIST
CT WARRANT MILITANTTE TECHNOGRAPHER ELECTRO
ROTELEPATH PREFECTI METATRON MUNITORI HEALER
ER PROCLAMATOR FAMULOUS DIALOGOUS ENFORCER
NIST MATERIUM ASPIRANT REDEMTIONIST REDEMPTORII
BERSEER BONESEER MUTANI DEATHE MASKA PSYKER
TUS TECHNOMAT TAROTSCRIOR DARK SCION MYSTIC
LPHAS ENSLAYER SCAVENGER COMMISSAR SCHOLE
EDICANTUS MENDICANTE REVISIONIST WATCHMAN
GALLOWGLASS FAUVILLE EXCRUCIATOR GOVENOR
MANCER STIRLITE HYPAPYSTON HAGG BOT NANOPHYLII
R SERVENTO LOGI VIGILODE IMPERORITE INQUISITOR
THCORE LEVINE CORTTEWAYNE ALCHEMIST STARKKYND
E ACCOKYTUS CUSTODIAN BLACK GUARD OVERLORD
GMAN CUTSTOVE HEADSMAN ADAPTII HENCHMAN
HRONO GLADIATOR PROPHECT SEER SAGE STEERSMAN
YKE CUTTAR PATHFINDER WAYSMITII JURYCANT LOCK
E TRADER DEATH CULTIST SUN SLINGER MULTICHMIST
KER NAVIGATOR MECHANIK RENEGADE TECHPRIEST
MAGES CARYATID TALLYMAN DESPERADO CONFESSOR
ASTER LEXOGRAPHER LOGISTER WARP STEALER INDITT
ST SOLAR PRIEST VYPERION CULT MECHAN TECH ADEPT
MITE CHAPLAIN DIOCESAN PRELATE PULPITEER SEXTANT
INNE MERCANTILIST JOURNEY MAN SARGEANT AT ARMS
ISTER DICISPLINATOR APOSTATE NOMAD HIVER SHADOW

OMNISSIAH MAGOS BLESSED ALCHEMY ORDINAT
THAUMATURGE WARLOCK JUSTICAR OBSCURINE ADJU
PRIEST MECH DEACON POTENTIATE CONFEDERATE A
PHYSISCIA INTERROGATER PUPPETEER DRONE TARGE
REGULATOR PROCTOR MARSHALL LORD HIGH LORD ARC
NEONATE SANCTIONITE MECHWRIGHT ENGINSEER
SCOURGE KYNG DESPERADO THRONE AGENT PREFE
WARRIOR FAMILIAR SAVANT WARPSEER EXPLICATOR
PROGENUMATE CREEDYTE ORATOR SUPPLICANTER
GARROWGATOR HARROWHOUND CATAPHRACTU
XENOSTERENNE NEUROMAUNCHER DIGI MAUNCER XEN
STROOGEMENNE BRETHRENDAE ANCHORITE ADORA
PURITAN ACOLYTE RADICAL ASSASSIN JUDGE ARBITES D
GUNNJAK HOBBLON PYCKESPUR SLAYER SHACKLEMO
CHIROGEONNE GREY GUARDIAN EXECUTIONER HA
HIEROPHANT ARGOFLAGGELLANT STAGLOSSI CRUCIBLAS
AELMJAK BOG FERREL NIGHT CUR WEAPONSMITH SUNN
STAUNCH CRUSADER ZEALOT KEY KEEPER MALLEON RO
BOUNTY HUNTER HYRDMANNE ASTROPATH ASTOSI
MECHONPERITTE REPENTIANS BURNING MARTYR ARC
SEVITOR SERVADON DUELIST CLERIC ARBITRATOR LOR
CHIRUGEON SCRIBE SCRIVONOR MISSIONARY HELIO PI
CABALYTE ADJUNDANT ANNIHALATOR ILLUMINATOR HI
SKINNER XENOGRAPHER BATTLE BISHOP GUILDER FREE
THYBILANT PILGRIM HADIANT APOSTICATOR SORORITAN